EDINBUGGERS

VS.

WEEGIES

Why Edinburgh
is Slightly Superior to Glasgow

EDINBUGGERS START HERE

First published 2003
by Black & White Publishing Ltd
29 Ocean Drive, Edinburgh EH6 6JL

Reprinted 2003, 2004 (twice), 2005, 2008

ISBN 978 1 902927 92 3

British Library Cataloguing in Publication Data:
A catalogue record for this book is available
from the British Library.

Printed and bound by Norhaven A/S

INTRODUCTION

Diligent readers will notice that this section is shorter than the Weegies one. Weegies talk a lot more.

The slogan: 'Glasgow's Miles Better' had only been in existence for about a minute when an Edinburgh wag asked: 'Than what? The Black Hole of Calcutta?' The song below is sung in Edinburgh, and not just at the football. I've heard it sung in pubs late of an evening, when the beer is revealing the real feeling.

To the tune of 'You Are My Sunshine':

> *You're just a Weegie*
> *A smelly Weegie*
> *You're only happy on Giro day*
> *Your Ma's a stealer*
> *Your Da's a dealer*
> *Please don't take my hubcaps away.*

Don't expect niceness within. Or much friendliness. 'Pal' is the unfriendliest word that there is in Glasgow. When a Weegie asks, in that Neanderthal accent: 'Ur you lookin' at me, pal?', you would be very naive indeed to think of it as a question, or that the

3

deliverer is intent on making friends. It is in fact a statement, meaning something like: 'Unless you come up with a smart reply sharpish, I am going to attempt to remove your head from your shoulders with any weapon that comes to hand. Or my teeth.'

Edinbuggers know that in Weegie families, father, mother and sister often don't add up to three, but that they do keep their chibs sharp, whatever a chib might be.

These are hard hits from the East side, digs, pokes in the eye, sharp jibes and bludgeoning diatribes, but it's just friendly rivalry really.

To again use the double positive negative, a figure of speech unique to Scotland:

Aye, right.

1
ATTITUDES AND INSULTS

An Edinbugger, a Fettes ex-pupil, says that though he could buy a mansion in Glasgow and have a million or so left over by moving there, he wouldn't want to live in a city where, more often than not, the school uniform is wellies.

True tale from an Edinburgh pavement cafe. Edinbugger: 'It's a real shame that those ETA terrorists are bombing the Weegies in Benidorm.'

Weegie at next table: 'But Edinbuggers go to Benidorm as well.'

Edinbugger: 'Not during the Glasgow Fair we don't.'

The question 'What school did you go to?' has different meanings in Glasgow and Edinburgh.

In Edinburgh the wrong answer can lead to social exclusion. In Glasgow it can lead to hospital inclusion.

Wee Weegie wumman: 'Ah'm sorry, son, ah canny cut ye a piece. Yer da's away tae the fitba wi' the breid knife.'

How do you know when you're staying in a hotel in Glasgow? When you call the receptionist and say 'I've got a leak in my sink' and the response is 'Aye fine, go ahead.'

In Edinburgh tables and chairs outside means a chance to have a seat and a chat over your coffee or beer. In Glasgow, it's a warrant sale.

Edinburgh is so middle class and middle of the road it should be called White Line City. It would also make it cosier-sounding and more like home for the junkies.

On the train from Glasgow to Edinburgh, a Weegie was berating the Edinbugger sitting across from him in the compartment. 'You Edinbuggers are too stuffy. You set yourselves apart too much. You think your stiff upper lips and your public schools make you above the rest of us. Takes you five generations to accept an immigrant.

'Look at me and my brothers and sisters. We have Italian blood, Russian blood, Jewish blood, Danish blood and Swedish blood. What do you say to that?'

The Edinbugger replied, 'Your mother sounds like a very sporting lady.'

THE DAY THE BUCKY THRIVED

Long, long time ago, I can still remember how those
                    Weegie bampots made me laugh,
And I know if I had a chance to see those Neds and
                    Sengas dance,
I'd laugh my arse off once again.
'Cos don't they realise it's not clever,
Drinking Buckfast doon the river,
Tucked-in tracky bottoms,
They look just fucking rotten!
I can't remember if I cried when I saw these bams in
                    East Kilbride,
But it amused me deep inside, the day the Bucky thrived!
And they were singin' . . .

Bye, bye, eatin' Greggs' cheapest pie,
Drove the Uno roon' the toon oh wi' the techno up high,
Wearing pure wool bunnets though it's nearly July
Singin', 'There's that posh wee c*** fae Milngavie!
'There's that posh wee c*** fae Milngavie!'

Did you write the book of shite?
'Gonnae geez ten bob, gonnae gee'za light?'

Get tae fuck, yer full o' pish!
Oh and do you believe in hard-core techno?
Huv ye gubbed five eccies fur a night at the Metro?
And can you teach me how to speak reeeaaallll fast?!
You can tell that she's in love wi' him,
Cos he's a Brig'ton Billy and she's a Tim,
They kicked off filthy socks and those manky old
Reeboks.
He was a scrawny youth with a GAP pullover,
A sovvy ring and a stolen Nova,
They fell in love when he muff doved 'er,
The day the Bucky thrived . . .

And they were singin' . . .
Bye bye, eatin' Greggs' cheapest pie
Drove the Uno roon' the toon oh wi' the techno up high,
Wearing woolly bunnets though it's nearly July
Singin', 'There's that posh wee c*** fae Milngavie!

'There's that posh wee c∗∗∗ fae Milngavie!'

Now for ten years you've been on the dole,
Hingin' aboot at the Paisley Toll,
And that's just how it's always been.
When the heidcase screamed at the polis van,
In a coat he'd stolen fae Top Man,
And a fag that came from you or me
But while the cop was looking dapper,
The wee bam chibbed him on the napper,
Dressed all in Kappa clobber,
As he shouted, 'Suck ma dobber!'
While wee Tam stole shoes fae Clarks',
And Boab slashed some c∗∗∗ in the park,
They all buzzed petrol in the dark,
The day the Bucky thrived . . .

And they were singin' . . .
Bye bye, eatin' Fray Bentos pie
Drove the Uno roon' the toon oh wi' the techno up high
Wearing woolly bunnets though it's nearly July
Singin', 'There's that posh wee c∗∗∗ fae Milngavie!
'There's that posh wee c∗∗∗ fae Milngavie!'

Helter skelter, if the wean greets belt 'er
Writing mentions on the old bus shelter,
Eight days straight drinking Faaaaaaaaaast!

9

Doin' six month for selling smack,
The chip pan diet and the heart attack
A night out at Archaos wi' the burd.
The Sengas reek of cheap perfume,
While name-tags jangle round the room,
Each one grabs her geezer,
A fag and lemon Breezer.
The lack of class is hard to hide,
They cannae wait to get inside,
A stairheid winch and a doorway ride,
That's how the punters thrive.

And they were singin' . . .
Bye bye, eatin' Greggs' cheapest pie
Drove the Uno roon' the toon oh wi' the techno up high,
Wearing woolly bunnets though it's nearly July
Singin', 'There's that posh wee c*** fae Milngavie!
'There's that posh wee c*** fae Milngavie!'

You'll see them in their usual places,
With silly hats and ugly faces,
Ootside the offy acting hard.
So Shug be nimble, Shug be quick,
And get an ounce of speed on tick
Then cut it up and sell it to yer pals.
All lined up ootside the 'Paki's',
A rainbow of exotic trackies,

Giein' abuse tae grannies,
Ya fucked-up bunch of fannies!
And as the day turns in to night,
The Neds may gang up to start a fight,
But on their own they're soft as shite!
That day the Old Firm tied.

And they were singin' . . .
Bye bye, eatin' Greggs' cheapest pie
Drove the Uno roon' the toon oh wi' the techno up high,
Wearing woolly bunnets though it's nearly July
Singin', 'There's that posh wee c*** fae Milngavie!
'There's that posh wee c*** fae Milngavie!'

(Slowly, with feeling)

I met a girl who sang 'The Sash', I asked about her pant
                                                    moustache,
But she just told me to fuck off!
I went down to the local chippy,
Where the Neds hung out and the staff were nippy,
And the punters there harassed me for some fags.
Baseball hats at stupid angles,
The girls each wore three-dozen bangles,
Hair done up with scrunchies,
Munching crisps and Crunchies.
But the three meals they enjoy the most,

Are cocks, chippies, beans on toast,
Come Glasgow Fair they hit the coast,
Those days the Bucky thrives!

And they were singin' . . .
Bye bye, eatin' Greggs' cheapest pie
Drove the Uno roon' the toon oh wi' the techno up high,
Wearing woolly bunnets though it's nearly July
Singin', 'There's that posh wee c*** fae Milngavie!
'There's that posh wee c*** fae Milngavie!'

Before the last World Cup, a primary school teacher in Edinburgh asked her pupils if they wanted to see England win it. The whole class put their hands up except for one girl who said she wanted Sweden, Argentina or Nigeria to win. Amazed, the teacher asked why. 'Well, Miss, my mum and dad are Scottish so I'm a Scotland fan too.' The teacher replied: 'You don't have to be a Scotland fan because your parents are; if your mum was a prostitute and your dad was a junkie that stole and beat up innocent people you wouldn't be like that.'

'No, Miss,' the girl said, 'that would make me a Weegie.'

Two boys are playing football in the Meadows when suddenly one of them is attacked by a Rottweiler.

Thinking quickly, his friend rips a plank of wood from a fence, forces it into the dog's collar and twists it, breaking the dog's neck.

All the while, a journalist from the *Scotsman* who was taking a stroll through the park is watching. He rushes over, introduces himself and takes out his pad and pencil to start his story for the next edition. He writes: 'Brave Hibs fan saves friend from vicious animal!'

The boy interrupts: 'But I'm not a Hibs fan.' The reporter starts again: 'Hero Hearts fan rescues friend from horrific attack!'

Again the boy interrupts: 'But I'm not a Hearts fan either.'

'Who do you support then?' inquires the reporter. 'Celtic,' comes the reply.

So the reporter starts again:

'Weegie bastard murders family pet.'

Your average Glaswegian is a sort of one-man or one-woman slum. Inside and out.

To the tune of 'Mistletoe and Wine':

DREAMING OF A WEEGIE CHRISTMAS

Christmas time, drunkenness and crime,
Children playing in filth and grime,
With cars on fire and trainers under tree
Time to rejoice in be-ing Weegie,
It's a time for stealing, a time for receiving,
Knock-off gear – worra great feelin'
Why pay top dollar, yer can nick it for free,
Just like our 'lecky, gas and TV.

Christmas time, piss-ups all the time
Nicking ciggies, spirits and wine
Wearing shell-suits and Nikes – all knocked-off gear
It's great getting pissed – on someone else's beer.

Its a time for drinkin', six packs of Stella
That ye got from some dodgy fella
Christmas is sound, Christmas is best
God bless our dealer – and the DHSS
Christmas time, time to joy-ride
Then go and visit family inside
With Dad on a six stretch and Sis up the duff
This 'City of Culture' can get pretty rough.

So next time you're driving through Weegie-city
You may just know why the streets look so shitty
So keep a sharp eye out for those dodgy deals
If you park for two minutes, they're off with your
wheels.

Edinburgh saying: Laugh alone and the world thinks you're an idiot.

Sean Connery was interviewed by Michael Parkinson, and bragged that despite his 72 years of age, he could still have sex five times a night. Lulu, who was also a guest, looked intrigued. After the show, Lulu said, 'Sean, if Ah'm no bein' too forward, Ah'd love tae huv sex wi an aulder man. Let's go back tae mah place.' So they go back to her place and have great sex. Afterwards, Sean says, 'If you think that was good, let me shleep for half an hour, and we can have even better shex. But while I'm shleeping, hold my baws in your left hand and my wullie in your right hand. Lulu looks a bit perplexed, but says, 'Okay.' He sleeps for half an hour, awakens, and they have even better sex. Then Sean says, 'Lulu, that was wonderful. But if you let me shleep for an hour, we can have the besht shex yet. But again, hold my baws in your left hand, and my wullie in your right hand.' Lulu is now used to the routine and complies. The results are mind blowing. It happens five times. Once it's all over, and the cigarettes are lit, Lulu asks, 'Sean, tell me, dis mah haudin' yer baws in mah left hand and yer wullie in mah right stimulate ye while ye're sleepin'?'

Sean replies, 'No, it's just that the lasht time I shlept with a Glashwegian, she shtole my wallet.'

Sean Connery has fallen on hard times. All work has dried up and he's just sat at home twiddling his thumbs. Suddenly the phone ring and Sean answers it. It's his agent and Sean gets very excited. The agent says, 'Sean, I've got a job for you. Starts tomorrow, but you've got to get there early, for 10ish.'

Sean frowns and replies, '10-ish? But I haven't even got a racket.'

2
GLASGOW TO HOST 2008 OLYMPICS

In an attempt to influence the members of the international Olympic Committee on their choice of venue for the games, the organisers of Glasgow's bid have drawn up an itinerary and schedule of events. A copy has been leaked and is reproduced below.

Opening Ceremony – The Olympic flame will be ignited by a petrol bomb thrown by a native of the city (probably from the Easterhouse area), wearing the traditional costume of shell suit, baseball cap and balaclava mask. It will burn for the duration of the games in a large chip van situated on the roof of the stadium.

The Events – In previous Olympic games, Scotland's competitors have not been particularly successful. In order to redress the balance, some of the events have been altered slightly to the advantage of local athletes:

100-Metre Sprint – Competitors will have to hold a video recorder and microwave oven (one under each arm) and on the sound of the starting pistol, a police dog will be released from a cage 10 yards behind the athletes.

100-Metre Hurdle – As above but with added obstacles (i.e. car bonnets, hedges, garden fences, walls etc.).

Hammer – Competitors may choose the type of hammer they wish to use (claw, sledge, etc) the winner will be the one who can cause the most grievous bodily harm to members of the public within the time allowed.

Fencing – Entrants will be asked to dispose of as much stolen silver and jewellery as possible in five minutes.

Shooting – A strong challenge is expected from the local men in this event. The first target will be a moving police car, the next a post office van and then a Securicor wages vehicle.

Boxing – Entry to the boxing will be restricted to husband-and-wife teams, and will take place on a Friday night. The husband will be given 15 pints of Tennents lager while the wife will be told not to make him any tea when he gets home. The bout will then commence.

Cycling Time Trials – Competitors will break into the University bike sheds and take an expensive mountain bike owned by some mummy's boy from the country on his first trip away from home. All against the clock.

Cycling Pursuit – As above, but the bike will belong to a visiting member of the Australian rugby team who will witness the theft.

Modern Pentathlon – Amended to include mugging, breaking and entering, flashing, joy-riding and arson.

The Marathon – A safe route has yet to be decided, but competitors will be issued with bags full of litter which they will distribute on their way round the course.

Swimming – Competitors will be thrown off the Clyde Suspension Bridge. The first three survivors back will decide the medals.

Men's 50-Km Walk – Unfortunately this event will have to be cancelled as police cannot guarantee the safety of anyone walking the streets of Glasgow.

Closing Ceremony – Entertainment will include formation rave dancing by members of Glasgow Health in the Community anti-drug campaigners, synchronised rock throwing and music by the Govan Boys Band. The Olympic flame will be extinguished by someone dropping an old washing machine onto it from the top floor of the block of flats next to the stadium. The stadium will then be boarded up before the local athletes break into it and remove all the copper piping and the central heating boiler.

Jimmy the Weegie was awarded £10,000 for injuries received after a traffic accident and his wife got £2,000. A friend asked how badly injured his wife had been in the accident. He replied 'She wasn't hurt at all but I had the presence of mind to break her leg before the polis arrived.'

3
ARE YOU LIVING TOO CLOSE TO GLASGOW?

Below are some tell-tale signs:

1. Your spouse has a poster of Andy Goram smiling.

2. You let your twelve-year-old daughter smoke at the dinner table in front of her kids.

3. You've been married three times and still have the same in-laws.

4. You think that a woman is 'out of your league' because she asks for a glass with her Tennents Super.

5. The phrase 'Thunderbirds are go!' reminds you the off-license has just opened.

6. You wish your toilet at home could be as clean as the one in the bus station.

7. At least one member of your family has died right after saying, 'Hey! Watch this.'

8. You think Dom Perignon is a Mafia leader.

9. Your wife's hairdo is ruined by a ceiling fan.

10. Your school had a students' creche.

11. One, or more, of your kids was born on a pub pool table.

12. One, or more, of your kids was conceived on a pub pool table.

13. Your back door coal bunker is ideal for the Rottweiler to raise its pups.

14. The trade-in value of your Transit goes up and down, depending on how full the tank is.

15. You don't have to leave the house to put rubbish in the wheelie bin.

16. You once lit a match in the bathroom and the windows blew out.

17. You only need one more stamp on your card to get a freebie at Tam's Tattoos.

18. You can't get married to your childhood sweetheart because of the current bestiality laws.

19. You think 'loading a dishwasher' means getting your wife drunk.

20. Your toilet paper has page numbers on it.

and finally . . .

21. The soundtrack on your wedding video ends with the loudhailer message: 'THIS IS THE POLICE'.

Santa Claus, the tooth fairy, an intelligent Weegie and an old drunk are walking down the street together when simultaneously they each spot a £50 note.
    Who gets it?
    The old drunk, of course. The other three are mythological.

A father takes his young son to the zoo. They are fascinated by the lions. 'Daddy, Daddy, why is that lion licking his bum?' asks the wee boy.

'Son, that's because he's just eaten a Weegie and is trying to get rid of the taste.'

Signs You've Been in Glasgow Too Long

1. You say 'pish' all the time.

2. You say 'aye' all the time.

3. You end sentences with 'like' i.e. 'I'm no goin' there, like. It's pish.'

4. You think McEwans beer is great, ignoring the fact it 'tastes of pish, like.'

5. You get an urge to punch everybody you meet.

6. You punch everybody you meet.

7. You get drunk before, after and during punching everybody you meet.

8. You are incomprehensible.

9. People seem to be scared of you when you say where you are from.

10. You automatically get the urge to kill on hearing the words 'Edinburgh' or 'England'.

11. You have heart disease aged 26 due to all the deep-fried pizzas you have consumed since birth.

The Edinbugger bus driver was giving a tour of Edinburgh to a group of tourists. The tour went round the town and the driver would point out sights of interest, particularly rugby playing fields. He drove past one area and said, 'Over there is where Wanderers PULVERIZED the Weegies.' They drove on a little further and the driver pointed to another field along the roadway and said, 'This is the place where Stewarts Melville MASSACRED Jordanhill.' Not much further down the road the driver told his passengers that on the right was the great field where Edinburgh WHIPPED the Hawks.

About that time a man on the bus, with a broad Weegie accent, said, 'Haw, didn't the Glaswegians win any games around here?'

The response was: 'Not when I'm driving the bus.'

Edinbugger to Weegie: 'You are depriving some poor village of its idiot.'

The purchasing agent of a big company was a stuffy old Edinbugger, but he gave an extensive order to a Weegie salesman. Although he had won the business in open competition, the salesman was grateful at being chosen and sought a way to show it.

He knew he daren't offer the buyer a commission, and a gift of money, he thought, would be regarded by him as an insult. The man, he noticed, constantly smoked cigars. So the salesman slipped out to a cigar shop and bought a box of fifty of the finest Havanas the tobacconist had. The price for the fifty was £500, but it had been a really big order that he had won. He brought the box back and asked the buyer to accept it with his compliments.

The latter explained that it was against company policy for its buyers to accept presents of any sort from those with whom the concern did business. He was sorry, he said, but he could not take the cigars as a present, even though he felt sure his young friend had tendered them with the best of intentions and in absolute good faith.

The young Weegie had another idea:

'Well,' he said, 'I hate to throw these cigars away. They are no use to me – I don't even smoke cigarettes. I wonder if you would buy them from me? There's no harm in that, surely.'

'What would you be asking for them?' inquired

the Edinbugger.

'I'll sell the whole fifty to you for a fiver,' stated the salesman.

The buyer lifted one of the cigars from the top row, smelled it, rolled it in his fingers and eyed it closely.

'Okay,' he said, 'at that price I'll take four boxes.'

Edinburgh threat: I'll wring your neck, ya wee Weegie bastard, but only if you wash it.

Alex McLeish was looking to sign some new players to help Rangers title push, so he sent his chief scout to Iraq to search for some new talent. Sure enough, the scout finds an outstanding eighteen-year-old striker and immediately signs him on a three-year deal.

On getting back to Scotland, McLeish takes one look at him in training and immediately puts him in the starting line up for the big away game against Celtic.

The new lad is fantastic, he scores a hat trick and creates four more as Rangers romp it 7–0. Ecstatic after the game, the young lad phones his mum to tell her the good news.

'Mum,' he says, 'I've just made my debut and had a great game. The team loves me, the fans love me and the press loves me, even them twats on the Radio Clyde phone-in love me. Life is great!'

'Well,' says his mum, 'I'm glad life is great for you. Shall I tell you what happened to us today? Your dad's been murdered in the street, your sister and I were raped and beaten in broad daylight, and your brother's joined a vicious gang of killers.'

'Mum, I don't know what to say. I'm so sorry.'

'Sorry?' she yells down the phone. 'You're fucking sorry? It's your fucking fault we moved to Glasgow in the first place!'

Badge spotted in one of Glasgow's fine call centres: 'I'm just working here until a good fast-food job opens up.'

How many Weegie flies does it take to screw in a light bulb?

Only two, but you have to wonder how the sneaky wee bastards got in there.

How many Glasgow rugby fans does it take to change a light bulb?

Seven – one to change it, five to moan about it and the coach to say that if the ref had done his job in the first place the light bulb would never have gone out.

Weegie teachers are known to use the following euphemisms on pupils' report cards:

'A born leader' – Runs a protection racket

'Easy-going' – Bone idle

'Good progress' – You should have seen him a year ago

'Friendly' – Never shuts up

'Helpful' – A creep

'Reliable' – Informs on his friends

'Expresses himself confidently' – Cheeky wee bastard

'Enjoys physical education' – A bully

'Does not accept authority easily' – Dad is in prison

'Often appears tired' – Stays up all night watching television

'A rather solitary child' – He smells

'Popular in the playground' – Sells pornography to his pals

Glaswegians are so lazy that they won't marry a woman till she's pregnant.

How do you make a Ouija board? Take away his jellies and his heroin.

4
EDINBUGGERS AND DRINK

Jock the Edinbugger reckoned he was a great judge of a glass of whisky – and a merciless executioner.

Sandy the Edinbugger was sitting at the bar drinking double whiskies in one gulp as fast as the barman could put them in front of him. He eventually explained that it was the only way he could drink them after a terrible accident. 'What sort of accident?' asked the barman. 'Terrible,' said Sandy. 'I knocked one over with my elbow.'

'The Scotch [sic] do not drink . . . During the whole of two or three pleasant weeks spent lecturing in Edinburgh, I never on any occasions saw whisky made use of as a beverage. I have seen people take it, of course, as a medicine, or as a precaution, or as a wise offset against a rather treacherous climate; but as a beverage, never.'

Stephen Leacock, author and humourist

The minister of a church in one of the more salubrious districts of Edinburgh was preaching a strong sermon about the evils of drink, and kept telling the congregation not to imbibe too frequently. He concluded:

'We'll not make this sermon too personal, but if a short, bald-headed chap who owns a chain of video shops, two restaurants and a pub, and is sitting in the corner of the east gallery pew, takes it to heart, then the Lord surely does work in mysterious ways.'

The old Edinbugger was asked by a friend what he thought of his nearest neighbour. He replied:

'Och, weel, he's a decent-like lad, but he's no' exactly a temperance man. He was sittin' there juist drinkin' an' drinkin', until I could scarcely see him.'

The two old Edinburgh worthies had imbibed over-much. Saying his goodnight, the one told the other:

'John, man, when ye gang oot at the door, ye'll see twa cabs. Tak the first yin – the t'ither ane's no' there!'

EDINBUGGER SONG

Has Glasgow ever had a poet who was also a lawyer? Edinbuggers who turned up their noses at Duncan Macrae's singing of 'The Wee Cock Sparra' should be aware that it was written by an Edinbugger lawyer, Hugh Frater. Nobody who saw Duncan sing this will ever forget it. Here it is:

A wee cock sparra sat on a tree,
A wee cock sparra sat on a tree,
A wee cock sparra sat on a tree
Chirpin' awa as blithe as could be.

Alang came a boy wi' a bow and an arra,
Alang came a boy wi' a bow and an arra,
Alang came a boy wi' a bow and an arra,
And he said: 'I'll get ye, ye wee cock sparra.'

The boy wi' the arra let fly at the sparra,
The boy wi' the arra let fly at the sparra,
The boy wi' the arra let fly at the sparra,
And he hit a man that was hurlin' a barra.

The man wi' the barra cam owre wi' the arra,
The man wi' the barra cam owre wi' the arra,
The man wi' the barra cam owre wi' the arra,
And said: 'Ye take me for a wee cock sparra?'

The man hit the boy, tho he wasne his farra,
The man hit the boy, tho he wasne his farra,
The man hit the boy, tho he wasne his farra,
And the boy stood and glowered; he was hurt
                                        tae the marra.

And a' this time the wee cock sparra,
And a' this time the wee cock sparra,
And a' this time the wee cock sparra
Was chirpin awa on the shank o' the barra.

5
LEARN YOURSELF WEEGIE

'Yawright pal? How's it gaun?'
'Good day to you, gentlebeing. How rests the world with you? I trust that your heart is lightsome with content and gladness.'

'Wit ur you aw aboot?'
This phrase has a few meanings, among them: 'Pardon me awfully, but the semantic content of your statement eludes me,' and, 'Explain yourself in a decidedly speedy fashion or be prepared for a bout of fisticuffs.'

'It's pure Baltic, man'
To anyone who has stood at, say, just at random, a game of football in Lithuania (which is on the Baltic) where it is minus twelve degrees centigrade, with a wind-chill factor in the hundreds and sharp-edged hailstones drawing blood from your cheeks, this is self-explanatory.

'Ah'm Joe the toff. See youse the morra'
'Toodle pip, chaps, I'm leaving now. Words cannot explain my pain at this rude leavetaking, but I hope to have the infinite pleasure of remaking your acquaintance on the morrow.'

'You ur a pure steamer, by the way'
'Ah, a virgin alcoholic, by the roadside. That's you, that is.'

'Get oot ma face or yer malkied'
'At this point I am in danger of committing the solecism of a smidge of miffedness with your good self and may have to make it a requirement that you visit an establishment specialising in facial stitching, unless you depart at the toot.'

'Jimmy'
The name that you brought with you to Glasgow no longer exists. You are now called Jimmy. There is a Glasgow by-law which states that all first-born children are to be named Jimmy, though exemptions may be granted for girls not expected to live, so you are now one of us. Learn to love it.

Big Man/Wee Man

Upon meeting you a Glaswegian will instantly group you into the Big Man or Wee Man category. Do not dispute this judgement, as God has been wrong more often than your average Weegie at the height category placement gemme.

Hen/Doll

If you are male and another male calls you either of these, just glass the radge with no further ado, as he is at the kiddin' and swankin'. If you are female these soubriquets are acceptable and may lead to high-intensity peer bonding. A hen is almost invariably older than a doll. Do not dispute your classification.

6
LITERARY FIGURES AND OTHERS

The impression Edinburgh has made on me is very great; it is quite beautiful, totally unlike anything that I have ever seen; and what is more, Albert, who has seen so much, says that it is unlike anything he ever saw.

Queen Victoria: *Letters*

Who indeed, that has once seen Edinburgh, with its couchant lion crag, but must see it again in dreams, waking or sleeping?

Charlotte Bronte

This braw, hie-heapit toun.

Lewis Spence: *The Prows o' Reekie*

And though I would rather die elsewhere, yet in my heart of hearts I long to be buried among good Scots clods. I will say it fairly, it grows on me with every year: there are no stars as lovely as Edinburgh streetlamps. When I forget thee, Auld Reekie, may my right hand forget its cunning!

> Robert Louis Stevenson,
> writing in *The Scot Abroad*

Glasgow is one of the few places in Scotland which defy personification . . . The monster of Loch Ness is probably the lost soul of Glasgow, in scales and horns, disporting itself in the Highlands after evacuating finally and completely its mother-corpse.

> Lewis Grassic Gibbon: *Scottish Scene*

The majority of Glasgow pubs are for connoisseurs of the morose, for those who relish the element of degradation in all boozing . . . It is the old story of those who prefer hard-centred chocolates to soft, storm to sunshine, sour to sweet. True Scots always prefer the former of these opposites.

> Hugh MacDiarmid: *The Dour Drinkers of Glasgow*

E megliore avere una morta nella casa che un Edinborgese alla porta. *It is better to have a dead man in your house than an Edinburgh man at your door.*

> A Florentine

(What did Edinburgh do to annoy Florence?)
Thanks to the ladies of the *Herald* Library for duties above and beyond with this.

Glasgow, that damned sprawling evil town.
> G.S. Fraser: *Meditations of a Patriot*

The accent of the lowest state of Glaswegians is the ugliest one can encounter. It is associated with the unwashed and the violent.
> Anonymous university lecturer, quoted by Janet Menzies in *Investigation of Attitudes to Scots and Glaswegian Dialect Among Secondary School Pupils*

He has not the brains of a Glasgow baillie.
> Herbert Asquith on Andrew Bonar Law

Edinburgh's much-quoted and vainglorious title: 'The Athens of the North', is turned on its head by playwright Tom Stoppard. He calls it: 'The Reykjavik of the South'.

7
JUST DESERTS

An Edinbugger and a Weegie are walking along a beach, when they see an old bottle. The Weegie picks it up and takes out the cork.

Out pops a genie who says, 'I am the genie with the light brown hair. I will grant you three wishes each.'

Wish 1 – 'OK, then,' the Weegie says, 'I wish every person in Glasgow was female apart from me.'

Wish 1 – 'I'd like a Ferrari,' says the Edinbugger.

Wish 2 – The Weegie, wanting better than the Edinbugger, says, 'I wish everyone in Europe was female apart from me.'

Wish 2 – 'I'd like a garage for my Ferrari,' says the Edinbugger.

Final wish – 'I wish everyone in the world was female apart from me,' says the Weegie.

Final wish – 'I wish the Weegie to be gay!' says the Edinbugger.

Edinburgh prayer: 'God bless Edinburgh. And God, we've got to flit to Glasgow tomorrow. So, goodbye, God.'

8
THIEVING WEEGIES

If you see a Weegie on a bicycle, why should you never swerve to hit him?

It could be your bike.

An Edinbugger woman said that whenever someone from Edinburgh wears something expensive, it looks old, and when a Weegie does so, it looks stolen.

What is the difference between Batman and a Weegie?

Batman can go out without robbin'.

What did the little Weegie boy get for Christmas?

Your bike.

9
STUPID WEEGIES

A scientist is researching the effects of the loss of brain power on people's speech.

He brings in a guy off the street to participate in the experiments.

As they attach the electrodes to his head, the guy says, 'May I please have a drink of water?'

But the scientist ignores him and says to his assistant, 'Remove 25 per cent of his brain power now.'

The assistant does this and the guy then says, 'Give me water.'

Again the scientist ignores him and says: 'Remove another 25 per cent.'

Guy: 'Give drink water.'

Scientist: 'Now another 25 per cent.'

Guy: 'Wawa, wawa.'

Scientist: 'And now, the final 25 per cent.'

Guy (singing): 'I belong to Glasgow . . .'

A Weegie was out for a walk and came to a river and saw an Edinbugger on the opposite bank. 'Hello there,' she shouts, 'how can I get to the other side?' The Weegie looked up the river, then down the river, then shouted back, 'You ARE on the other side.'

The young Weegie's report card said: 'At last some good news. We thought Hamish had reached rock bottom. But now he has developed a hitherto unsuspected talent for digging.'

Sandy and his friend Angus lived in identical tenement flats in Glasgow. One night at the pub Sandy mentioned he had just papered the kitchen. Angus said, 'I've been wanting tae dae that! How much paper did ye get?'

'Seven rolls,' said Sandy.

A week later they met again and Angus says, 'Here you! I had two and a half rolls of paper left over frae my kitchen.'

'Aye,' says Sandy, 'so did I.'

10
EDINBUGGER PHILOSOPHY

Edinburgh question: If you try to fail, and succeed, which have you done?

In Edinburgh they say: 'Opportunities are never lost; someone will always take the one you missed.' In Glasgow they say: 'Do you mean oppurchancities?'

A closed mouth gathers no feet, as they say in Edinburgh.

Edinburgh saying: Give me ambiguity or give me something else.

The Edinbuggers' way of saying 'No' is to start a conservation group.

11

HEAVEN

'Heaven seems no' a' that much better than Glasgow,' a Weegie is said to have confided, after death, to a friend who had died before him. 'Man, this isny Heaven,' replied his pal.

A man from Edinburgh, an Aberdeen loon and a Weegie wound up together at the Pearly Gates. St. Peter informed them that in order to get into Heaven, they would each have to answer one question.

St Peter addressed the Edinbugger and asked, 'What was the name of the ship that crashed into the iceberg?' He answered quickly, 'That would be the Titanic.' St Peter let him through the gate.

St Peter turned to the Aberdonian and, thinking that Heaven didn't need all the attitudes that this guy would bring with him, decided to make the question a little harder: 'How many people died on the ship?' Fortunately for him, he had seen the movie and answered, 'About 1,500.' 'That's right! You may enter.'

St Peter then turned to the Weegie: 'Name them.'

12
HELL

An Edinbugger, a Weegie and an Airdrieonian found themselves in Hell.

They were a little confused at their situation, and they were startled to see a door in the wall open. Behind the door was perhaps the ugliest woman they had ever seen. She was 3 ft 4 in., dirty, and you could smell her even over the brimstone.

The voice of the Devil was heard: 'Airdrieonian, you have sinned! You are condemned to spend the rest of eternity in bed with this woman!'

He was then whisked through the door by a group of lesser demons to his torment.

This understandably shook up the other two, and so they both jumped when a second door opened, and they saw an even more disgusting example of womanhood gone wrong. She was over 7 ft tall, monstrous, covered in thick black hair, and flies circled her.

The voice of the Devil was heard: 'Weegie, you have sinned! You are condemned to spend the rest of eternity in bed with this woman!' And he too was whisked off.

The Edinbugger, now alone, felt understandably anxious, and feared the worst when the third door opened. As it inched open, he strained to see the figure of . . . Cindy Crawford.

Delighted, the Edinbugger jumped up, taking in the sight of this beautiful woman, barely dressed in a skimpy bikini. Then he heard the voice of the Devil saying: 'Cindy, you have sinned . . . '

WEEGIES

VS.

EDINBUGGERS

**Why Glasgow
Smiles Better Than Edinburgh**

WEEGIES START HERE

First published 2003
by Black & White Publishing Ltd
29 Ocean Drive, Edinburgh EH6 6JL

Reprinted 2003, 2004 (twice), 2005, 2008

ISBN 978 1 902927 92 3

British Library Cataloguing in Publication Data:
A catalogue record for this book is available
from the British Library.

Printed and bound by Norhaven A/S

INTRODUCTION

There is a slogan that Glaswegians use when talking about Edinburgh's world-famous *joie de vivre*, which is: 'Edinburgh! A castle, a smile, and a song — one out of three isn't bad.' There is another faux (or foe) slogan: 'Edinburgh! It's Shooting Up', which conveys a little of how far a Weegie might be prepared to go to insult an Edinbugger. Or how about: 'Edinburgh! Salt, Sauce and Saunas!'

Within you will find the reasons why a Weegie would rather take Osama Bin Laden home for tea than an Edinbugger.

And of course traditionally there is no invitation to tea in Edinburgh, more of a statement, delivered without the question mark, as in: 'You'll have had your tea.'

These days, instead of the offer of a drink it is: 'You'll be driving.'

There's nothing rational about it. Weegies know that all Edinbuggers are just poncing about all day pretending to be flowers and waiting for dark to get up Calton Hill because, without exception, they like

3

their vice versa, and that people in Edinburgh equate breeding with good form, whereas in Glasgow they accept it as good fun.

There is a fairly prevalent paranoid myth among Edinbuggers that all Weegies want to move to Edinburgh and drive down property values, just out of badness. One Weegie woman summed up her feelings succinctly: 'I wouldn't want to move to a place where you have to put on matching clothing to pick up the milk from the doorstep.'

These are hard hits and sneaky bits from the West side, sharp jibes and bludgeoning diatribes, but it's just friendly rivalry really.

To use the double positive negative, a figure of speech unique to Scotland:

Aye, right.

1
GENERIC INSULTS

There are three kinds of people in Scotland.

First, there are the Edinbuggers. They keep the Sabbath – and everything else they can lay their hands on. They pray on their knees . . . and their neighbours.

Second, there are the Highlanders, who never know what they want, but are willing to fight for it anyway, in between complaints in very bad Gaelic.

Last, there are the Weegies, who consider themselves self-made men, thus relieving God of a terrible responsibility.

A quote from an economist who wishes to remain unidentified in case he becomes unidentified remains. 'Glasgow is still transfixed by its days of industrial and shipbuilding glory in the 19th century. Edinburgh is doing quite well in the 18th.'

2
ATTITUDES AND INSULTS

The standard disparagement of 'Fur coat and nae knickers' that is applied by the Weegie to the Edinbugger to illustrate the pretension to gentility so despised in the West is turned on its head by this tale of two girls going for a night out. One is from Glasgow, one is from Edinburgh.

Edinburgh girl says, 'Hang on a wee minute, I'll have to put on ma knickers.'

Glasgow girl looks shocked and says, 'Knickers! On a night oot?'

There are other Glasgow phrases that sum this up:
Curtains at the window and no sheets on the bed.
Pease brose and piannas.

Q: What do Edinbuggers use as
a form of contraception?
A: Their personalities.

Q: What do you do if you see an
Edinbugger with half a face?
A: Stop laughing and reload!

An Edinbugger, finally roused by a Weegie's needling, protested that he was born an Edinbugger and hoped to die an Edinbugger. 'Christ Almighty, man,' said the Weegie, 'have you no ambition at all?'

Weegies travel to Edinburgh, Edinbuggers make expeditions to Glasgow. And they are not tense while in Glasgow, just terribly, terribly alert.

Said by a Glasgow man of an unco guid Edinburgh man when informed of his demise, 'No doubt he'll get into heaven, but God won't like him. And it will be mutual.'

You get more laughs at a Glasgow funeral than at a wedding in Edinburgh.

In Edinburgh, about the only concession to gaiety is a striped shroud.

A Weegie girl and an Edinbugger guy are in a bar when the girl notices something strange about the wellies that the guy's wearing.

She says to him 'Excuse me, by the way, no bein' funny or that, but why does one of your wellies have an L on it, and the other one's got an R on it?'

The Edinbugger smiles, puts down his pint of Boggles Trout Piss and replies, 'Well, I am a little bit dense, you see. The one with the R is for my right foot and the one with the L is for my left foot.'

'Ya dancer!' exclaims the Weegie, 'So THAT'S why ma knickers have got C&A on them.'

The University of Edinburgh's Dr Graeme Ritchie, of the Institute for Communicating and Collaborative Systems in the Division of Informatics, is attempting to solve the riddle of how jokes work — and to set up a way of analyzing the language used in jokes — as part of wider research into humour. Dr Ritchie is not investigating how funny particular jokes are, as opinions about that vary widely. Instead, he is looking at whether something is or is not a

joke, about which there is more agreement.

Dr Ritchie's work is focused upon jokes, as they are small enough to describe easily, and tend to be self-contained. His research involves studying classes of jokes, refining the abstract concepts used to describe the data and developing ways to analyse the data based on these ideas. Existing concepts from theoretical linguistics would be used as basic notions to construct an account of humorous effects, and develop guidelines.

Supported by a fellowship from the Leverhulme Trust, Dr Ritchie will use methods previously employed in the study of linguistics, to look at the way jokes are constructed. He will draw upon material from joke books, the Internet and academic books and 'dismantle' jokes, rephrasing them to discover the linguistic features which make jokes work.

He added: 'Humour is complex, but largely unexplained behaviour. It has great importance in culture and society, but we do not know why it should have developed. The explanation is not obvious, as it might be in the case of a key human "drive", like the need to feed. Despite centuries of philosophical discussion, we are very far from having a full and complete theory of humour.

'Modern linguistics builds upon centuries of

detailed descriptive work, but humour research has very little analysed data on which to base theories. To make progress, research into humour has to take a similar step to linguistics, and we need to produce precise and detailed scientific accounts.

'The outcome of this research will be the creation of a theoretical framework, that is, a set of basic linguistic ideas and methods suitable for spelling out the mechanisms that underlie jokes. This will lay the foundations for further research, including psycholinguistic experiments,' said Dr Ritchie.

The good doctor has got to be joking. Only in Edinburgh. Maybe he should change his first name to M'bosa. That, incidentally, should Dr Ritchie be reading this, is a joke. Or it might be a psycho-linguistic experiment.

A Weegie woman driver is pulled over by a policeman on the way out of Edinburgh.

'Is there a problem, officer?'

'Yes madam, you were speeding. May I see your licence please?'

'I'd give it to you but I don't have one.'

'Don't have one?'

'No. Lost it after drink driving four times.'

'I see. May I see your vehicle registration papers please?'

'Naw. Can't do that either.'

'Why not?'

'Well . . . I stole this car.'

'Stole it?'

'Yes, after I killed and chopped up the owner.'

'You what?'

'Lost my temper. It was messy. His body is in a pile of plastic bags in the boot if you want to see.' The policeman looks at the woman for a second, then backs away to his car and calls for reinforcements. Within minutes there are more police cars circling them. A police sergeant approaches the car. He clears his throat, then calls to her, 'Madam, please step out of and away from your vehicle.'

She does so. 'Is there a problem, sir?'

'One of my officers told me that you have stolen this car and murdered the owner.'

'Murdered the owner?'

'Yes. Could you open the boot of your car please?'

She does, and they both look down into a dusty, empty space.

'Is this your car, madam?'

'Yes. Here are the registration papers.'

The sergeant scans through them and sees that they are in order.

'My officer claims you do not have a driving licence.'

The woman rummages through her bag then hands

her licence to the puzzled sergeant.

'Mrs Smith, my officer told me you didn't have a licence, that you stole this car, and that you murdered and dismembered the owner.'

'I'll bet the lying Lothian bastard told you I was speeding too!'

A young Edinbugger stockbroker makes a ton of dough from a somewhat dodgy deal and celebrates not being caught by going out and buying a brand-new Ferrari 550.

He takes it out for a spin and, intoxicated by the speed and handling, is nearly at the Glasgow end of the M8 before he looks out and notices where he is. Panicking slightly when he discovers that he has to get off the motorway in Weegieland to turn, he nevertheless does so and is stopped at a red traffic light.

An old Weegie on a moped pulls up next to him. The old man looks over the sleek, shiny car and asks, 'What kind of motor have you got there, son?'

The young man replies, 'A Ferrari 550 – it cost 100 grand.'

'That's a lot of cash,' says the old man. 'Why did it cost so much?'

'Because this car can do up to 220 miles an hour!' he says proudly.

The moped driver asks, 'Mind if I take a look inside?'

'No problem, just try not to breathe on the upholstery,' replies the owner. So the old man pokes his head in the window and looks around.

Then sitting back on his moped, the old man says, 'That's a pretty nice car you've got there, pal, but I think I'll stick with my moped. I've seen the day, though, when I would have given you a race.'

Just then, the light changes to green so the guy decides to show the old man just what his car can do. He shouts: 'Right, you Weegie coffin-dodger,' floors it, and within 15 seconds the speedometer reads 160 mph.

Suddenly, he notices a dot in his rear view mirror. It seems to be getting closer. He slows down to see what it could be and suddenly, whooooooosssshhhh! Something whips past him, going much faster.

'What could be going faster than my flying machine?' the young man asks himself. He floors the accelerator again and takes the Ferrari up to 200 mph. Then, up ahead of him, he sees that it is the old man on the moped.

Amazed that the moped could pass his Ferrari and just a little bit apprehensive about the insult, he

gives it some more welly and passes the moped at 210 mph. Whhhhoooooooossssssshhhh!!! He's feeling pretty good until he looks in his mirror and sees the old man gaining on him again.

Astounded by the speed of this old guy he floors the accelerator and takes the Ferrari all the way up to 220 mph. Not ten seconds later, he sees the moped bearing down on him again. The Ferrari is flat out and there's nothing he can do. He is shitting bricks by now, as he thinks that the Weegie is out for revenge.

Suddenly, the moped ploughs into the back of his Ferrari, demolishing the rear end. He skids to a halt as the car catches fire.

The young man jumps out, and unbelievably, the old man is still alive. He runs up to the mangled old guy and says, 'Oh my God! Is there anything I can do for you?'

The old man says: 'Before I burn to death, gonny unhook my fucking braces from your wing mirror!'

Every Weegie will tell you that Edinburgh is of course necessary, if only to prevent all of those railways and trains from ending up in the Firth of Forth.

Glasgow's kids are not better natural fighters than Edinburgh kids. It is just that they are better trained and have better weaponry.

How many Edinbugger graduates does it take to screw in a light bulb?
One: he stands still and the world revolves around him.

Tam the Weegie is up in court in Glasgow, after running down two Edinbuggers with his car. The judge says: 'Now we have heard the evidence given, have you anything to say before I pass sentence?'

'Well,' Tam says, 'I had been out for a drive and I was making my way home, doing 30 mph, minding the speed limit, when out from between two cars stepped these two people, and I hit them. One came through the windscreen, the other went over the hedge.'

The judge looks at Tam and says: 'We have heard all the eyewitness reports, would you like to try again and tell the court what happened?'

'Ok,' says Tam. 'Well, I was trying to get home for my tea, the traffic had been bad, got to an open bit of road, I might have been doing about 45 mph in

the 30 zone, when these two poofy-looking guys stepped out in front of me and I hit them. One came through the windscreen the other went over the hedge.'

'Getting a bit more like the evidence now,' says the judge. 'Would you like one more chance?'

'Oh God, ok,' says Tam. 'Right, I'd been at the Glasgow/Edinburgh game at Hughenden and the bastards beat us 27–0. I was pissed off, so I was belting along at 75 mph to get to the pub to drown my sorrows, when I see these two Edinburgh fans walking along in their poncy rugby shirts. So I think, right ya bass, mounted the pavement, chased them for a bit, then got the twats. One came through the windscreen and the other went over the hedge.'

'That's better,' says the judge. 'It's now my duty to pass sentence. We'll charge one with breaking and entering, and the other with leaving the scene of the crime.'

'Glasgow . . . no fur coat and no Harvey Nicks,' is Edinburgh's response to the perennial jibe from Weegies. The good news from Glasgow's point of view is that Harvey Nicks didn't do all that well and that Selfridge's chose to snub Edinburgh and open in Glasgow.

Little Weegie Tommy was sitting on a park bench on a day out in Edinburgh munching on one deep-fried Mars Bar after another. After the sixth one an Edinbugger on the bench across from him said, 'Son, you know eating all that fat and chocolate isn't good for you. It will give you acne, rot your teeth, and make you fat.'

Little Weegie Tommy replied, 'My grandfather lived to be 107 years old.'

The man asked, 'Did your grandfather eat six Mars Bars at a time?'

Little Weegie Tommy answered, 'No, he minded his own fucking business!'

3

SIGNS YOU'VE BEEN
IN EDINBURGH TOO LONG

You say 'how?' instead of 'why?' But not in public.

The thought of haggis, neeps and tatties does not disgust you, but you only eat it to be 'ethnic'. Normally it is caviar or nothing.

You think Glaswegians are unsavoury, but you've never met any as you are too scared to go to Glasgow after dark in case somebody steals one of your eleven mobile phones.

You think it is your God-given right to slag all the other Scottish cities.

You speak with a Morningside accent when sober . . . and then like a Leith dockworker when drunk.

You have whisky for breakfast.

You are strangely proud and protective of Irn-Bru.

You haven't noticed how sickly and horrible Irn-Bru is.

You know the difference between a McDonald and a McKenzie tartan.

You think paying £10 for a 3-minute cab ride is perfectly acceptable.

You sulk at the champagne being warm at Hogmanay.

You sulk if there are no after-club parties because you can't possibly go to bed before 11.30 a.m. the next day.

You sulk if you don't manage to spend £1000 on

your Jenners account card in your lunch hour.

In Edinburgh a dog can teach a boy many things – fidelity, perseverance, and to turn around three times before lying down, especially on Calton Hill.

In Edinburgh they say: 'If at first you don't succeed, redefine success.' In Glasgow they say: 'If at first you don't succeed, ah, fuck it.'

In Glasgow everyone can do one thing better than everybody else . . . It's usually reading their own handwriting on the confession.

A Weegie stood watching an Edinbugger fishing. He noticed that the man dipped his bait into a bottle by his side before each cast and was astounded to find that he had a dozen fine trout flapping on the bank beside him within five minutes. He became curious and went down to ask what his secret was.

'No secret, but just a bottle of 50-year-old malt. The fish just can't get enough of it.'

So the man rushed back to his place and got out

his own fishing rod. Oddly enough, he didn't have any 50-year-old malt to hand so he decided to try out some of his freshly bought bottle of Buckfast instead.

The next day the Edinbugger was walking alongside the river and met the man coming the other way with a salmon the size of a small elephant slung over his shoulder. He prudently restrained his natural curiosity regarding the existence of a fishing permit and said: 'Congratulations. I'm glad to see the single malt trick worked for you too.'

The Weegie grinned back and said: 'You should try the electric soup instead. When I got this fish out of the water it took me five minutes to get the worm to let go of his throat.'

After pulling a Weegie over for speeding, a member of Lothian's finest started to lecture him about his speed, pompously implying that the Weegie didn't know any better and trying to make him feel as uncomfortable as possible. He finally started writing out the ticket, but had to keep swatting at some flies buzzing around his head. The Weegie asked, 'Having some problems with circle flies there, are ye?'

The policeman paused to take another swipe and said, 'Well, yes, if that's what they are. I've never

heard of circle flies.'

The Weegie was pleased to enlighten the cop. 'Circle flies are most common on farms. They're called circle flies because you almost always find them circling the backside of a horse.'

The policeman continues writing for a moment, then says, 'Are you trying to call me a horse's arse?'

'Oh no, officer,' the Weegie replies. 'I have too much respect for your particular force for that.'

'Good job,' the cop says snidely, then goes back to writing him up.

After a long pause, the Weegie adds, 'Hard to fool thae flies, though.'

What's the difference between a Pilton man and a large pizza?

A large pizza can feed a family of four.

An Edinbugger, an Irishman, a Weegie and a Tory MSP were sharing a railway carriage.

The MSP was reading the *Daily Mail*, and after a time he sighed with exasperation, screwed his paper up into a ball and threw it into the waste basket. The other passengers were shocked and asked why he had done that. He said: 'Well, in this country,

opinions like those are ten a penny.'

The Edinbugger was drinking a whisky he had bought from the bar when a similar mood of exasperation seemed to descend on him and he threw the glass in the bin.

'Why did you do that?' asked the others. 'Well, in my salary bracket, whiskies like that are ten a penny.'

The journey continued and the Irishman began to get restless and flung his book to join the other discards.

'Before you ask,' he said, 'in my part of the world authors are ten a penny.'

The Weegie had been sitting quietly when he suddenly lunged forward, pinioned the Edinbugger and stuffed him headfirst into the bin.

'Why did you do that?' they asked him.

He said: 'Felt like it.'

This Edinbugger walks into a book shop. He asks the clerk, 'Can I have a play by Shakespeare?'

The assistant says: 'Of course, sir. Which one?'

The Edinbugger says, 'William.'

It is truly said (by a Weegie) that if all of the editions of all of the books about Harry Potter were laid end

to end, it would still be raining in Edinburgh.

Incidentally, it is a little-known fact that the best-selling author of the above has been known to take a drink. You can tell from her name, Jakie Rowling.

What they drink in Edinburgh a lot is advocaat, which sounds, looks and tastes like it has been distilled from the juice of the backbones of lawyers.

The phone rang in a Rose Street pub and the landlord answered it.

'This is the IRA,' the voice said. 'There's a bomb in your pub and you've got five minutes to get out.'

The owner put the phone down and went back to the bar.

'Last orders, everyone!' he shouted.

A bus carrying only ugly Edinbuggers and the only ugly Weegie crashes into an oncoming truck, and everyone inside dies. They then get to meet their Maker and, because of the grief they have experienced, he decides to grant them one wish each before they enter Paradise.

They're all lined up, and God asks the first one what the wish is.

'I want to be gorgeous,' he says, so God snaps his fingers and it is done.

The second one in line hears this and says: 'I want to be gorgeous too.'

Another snap of the fingers and the wish is granted. This goes on for a while, but when God is halfway down the line, the Weegie, who is the last in line, starts laughing.

When there are only ten people left, this guy is rolling on the floor, laughing his bahookie off.

Finally, God reaches the guy and asks him what his wish will be.

The Weegie calms down and says: 'Make them all ugly again.'

A Weegie was made ashamed of his accent when working in Edinburgh so he went south to get elocution lessons. He returned three years later, speaking perfect Queen's English, and went out to celebrate with a drink, walking into the first establishment he could find.

'I say, my good man,' his silky tones rang out, 'perhaps you could find me a bottle of chilled Bolly and one of your finest Havana cigars.'

'You're from Glasgow, aren't you?' said the proprietor.

'Good Lord, how ever did you possibly know,' said the stunned and aggrieved Weegie.

'Well, you see,' said the proprietor, 'this is a butcher's.'

The *Evening News* sent a reporter to interview the oldest man in Edinburgh, Cameron Snoddie.

'And exactly how old are you, Mr Snoddie?' asked the young reporter.

'One hundred and three years old today,' he croaked.

'And I'm sure you've seen a fair few changes in your time, sir.'

'I have indeed, son. And I've been against them all.'

A young Weegie couple went to visit an estate agent in Edinburgh. 'Right,' said the agent. 'Just tell me your starting price, then we'll all have a good laugh and take it from there.'

Edinburgh question: What do you do when you see an endangered animal that is eating an endangered plant?

Answer: Make sure that you don't make eye contact with anyone.

In Edinburgh, if a mute swears, his mother washes his hands with soap. In Glasgow they just give him the finger.

A Greyfriars Bobby is rhyming slang in Glasgow for jobbie.

Edinburgh folk are so narrow-minded that even when they get an idea it comes out neatly folded.

Edinburgh, where no shirt is too young to be stuffed.

You know that you are working for the Scottish Executive in Edinburgh:

When someone asks about what you do for a living, you lie.

You get really excited about a 2% pay raise.

Your biggest loss from a system crash is that you lose your best jokes.

Your supervisor doesn't have the ability to do your job.

You sit in a cubicle smaller than your bedroom cupboard.

Computer specialists know less about computers than your teenager.

Lunch is like another scheduled meeting, but shorter.

If you see a good-looking person, you know they are a visitor.

A business trip with uncompensated mandatory weekend travel is seen as a perk.

Although you have a telephone, pager, e-mail, fax, company distribution, mail and co-workers sitting right on the other side of the partition . . . communication is a continuing problem.

You know, and everyone that works with you knows, that your performance is superior, but 'satisfactory' is the highest level on the documented performance rating.

You work 200 hours for the £100 bonus and jubilantly say 'Oh great, thanks very much!'

When workers screw up they are transferred to another office to be someone else's problem; when management screws up they are promoted.

Your boss's favourite lines are 'when you get a few minutes', 'in your spare time', 'when you're free' and 'I have an opportunity for you'.

Training is something spoken about but never seen.

A holiday is something that you'll get next year . . . maybe.

The worst possible reputation comes from being the initiator of a complaint.

The war between Glasgow and Edinburgh will not determine who is right – only who is left. And it won't start with E.

As they say in Glasgow: 'Dear God, grant me patience, but get a move on, Big Man!'

Trying to find an honest man in Edinburgh is like trying to find a fart in a Jacuzzi.

A Weegie walks into a Southside bar and says 'Gies a triple whisky!' He quickly downs it and says 'Another!' Again he sinks it and demands 'Another!'

He keeps on drinking until, after his eighth, the barman says, 'Pal, you drink like you've got a problem. Do you want to talk about it?'

The guy says 'Ten years I've been with my wife, even though she's an Edinbugger. I left work early today, to surprise her. I came home to find her in bed with my best friend.'

'What did you say to them?' asks the barman.

'I told her to get back to Edinburgh, and I told him "Bad dog, bad dog!"'

The wee Weegie was through in Edinburgh for the night and was having a quiet pint. A live band filed in to the pub and started to play a selection of Hearts songs.

As tune followed tune, all in praise of the far-from-mighty Jam Tarts, he leaned over the bar and shouted in the barman's ear: 'Is it just all Hearts songs or does this baun play anything on request?' he asked. 'Oh aye, they do,' said the barman. 'That's great,' said the Weegie. 'Gonny ask them to go ootside and play peever?'

One of the Weegie pastimes is to visit Edinburgh to play a game called Spot the Scot. If you spot one you win and can go home immediately. Nobody has ever won.

Another slogan mooted for Edinburgh, with the Weegie pronunciation: 'Edinbra! It's Full of Tits.'

And another: 'Edinbra! It's Got its Knockers . . . and Every One of them is Right, apart from the Left Ones.'

On the question of hypocrisy, the Kirk and saunas, notorious Edinbugger brothel-keeper Dora Noyce said that her highest takings were always when the General Assembly of the Church of Scotland was in session.

The two Edinbugger school inspectors were in a scheme in Glasgow waiting for a taxi, having been daft enough to leave their car outside the school. They noticed a Fort Knox of a pub and took note of the rough hand-lettered sign on the door, which read: 'We huv plain drinks and we huv fancy drinks.'

Reading this, the two Easterners smirked at each other and went in, scuffing their feet through the sawdust on the floor. 'Last night's furniture,' said one, grinning condescendingly.

There was a wee barman with his back to them washing glasses, so they started talking. One of them, addressing space, said: 'Seeing that they serve fancy drinks here, I'll have a gin rickey, maybe with a smoked olive. What are you going to have?' he added, addressing his fellow would-be joker.

'Good choice,' said the other, 'I think I'll try a dry martini cocktail, made with French vermouth, and a spiced cocktail onion, one of the coloured ones. Pink, perhaps.'

Without shifting his position or lifting his eyes from his work the barman said: 'I can kick the arse of any given two Edinbuggering space-wasters in 11.2 seconds. That's ma record, but Ah know Ah can beat it wi' you two. And Ah huvny even turned roon yet.'

The time was in the early hours of a new day during the Festival; the place was the desk of a hotel; the principal character was a well-dressed Weegie in an alcoholic fog, who had picked up his reservation a few minutes earlier.

Now, well scooshed, he came stumbling down from the second floor and stood swaying slightly in front of the desk.

'Haw,' he said politely but thickly, 'gonny geez anurra room?'

'Well, sir,' stated the young Edinbugger, 'we're a little bit crowded, as it is the Festival, so I don't know whether I could shift you immediately. It's pretty late, you know.'

'M'sorry,' said the guest in a courteous but slightly louder voice, 'I repeat – gonny geez anurra room?'

'Isn't the room I gave you comfortable?' she asked.

'Sheems awrigh,' admitted the transient. 'Nev'less, neetaebe moved.'

'Well, what's the matter with your room?' de-manded the pestered woman.

The stranger bent forward, and, with that Weegie jailbird air of one imparting a secret, said to her in a husky half whisper:

'S'oan fire!'

4
THE EDINBURGH CHRISTMAS CAROL

Late last week, I was rushing around trying to get some last-minute shopping done. I was stressed out and not thinking very fondly of the Festive season right then. It was dark, cold, and wet as I was loading my car with gifts that I felt obliged to buy. I noticed that I was missing a receipt that I might need later. So, mumbling under my breath, I retraced my steps to Jenners entrance.

As I was searching the wet pavement for the lost receipt, I heard a quiet sobbing. The crying was coming from a poorly dressed boy of about 12 years old. He was short and thin. He had no coat and was just wearing a ragged flannel shirt to protect him from the cold night's chill. Oddly enough, he was holding a £100 note in his hand. Thinking that he had become separated from his parents in the busy shop, I asked him what was wrong. He told me his sad story. He said that he came from a large family. He had three brothers and four sisters. His father had died when he was nine years old. His mother was poorly educated and worked at two full-time jobs. She made very little to support her large family.

Nevertheless, she had managed to skimp and save £200 to buy her children Christmas presents. The young boy had been dropped off, by his mother, on the way to her second job. He was to use the money to buy presents for all his siblings and save just enough to take the bus home. He had not even entered the shop when an older boy grabbed one of the £100 notes and disappeared into the night.

'Why didn't you scream for help?' I asked.

The boy said, 'I did.'

'And nobody came to help you?' I wondered.

The boy stared at the pavement and sadly shook his head.

'How loud did you scream?' I inquired.

The soft-spoken boy looked up and meekly whispered, 'Help me!'

I realised that absolutely no one could have heard that boy cry for help.

So I grabbed his other £100 and ran to the car.

A Weegie designer, who has designs on moving to Edinburgh and wishes to remain anonymous (easy peasy lemon squeezy in Edinburgh, one would think) claims that Edinburgh women wear: 'Clothing that looks as if it was designed and made by people who

WHY GLASGOW SMILES BETTER THAN EDINBURGH

had had clothes described to them, but who had never seen any.'

Two Edinbugger ladies had been enticed to Glasgow for the sales and were resting their barking dogs in a tearoom, having spent two hours looking for the cheapest one. One said to the friendly wee waitress who asked what they wanted: 'None of your Glasgow banter, thanks, just tea, and I hope my cup is clean.'

The waitress bustled off and returned with a pot of tea a moment or so later, saying cheerily: 'Which wan o' ye wanted the clean cup?'

Edinburgh is a terrible place for last names as first names. The only other place like it in Scotland is the BBC. Nobody is called Tam, Wullie or Davie. It is all: 'Oh Cameron, Munro would like a word. It's about Maxwell and McGregor wanting to change their names back to Shuggie and Duggie. Farquarson will never allow it.'

Q: What's the difference between Edinbuggers and a jet engine?
A: A jet engine eventually stops whining.

A man walking along a road in the countryside comes across a shepherd and a huge flock of sheep. Tells the shepherd, 'I will bet you £100 against one of your sheep that I can tell you the exact number in this flock.' The shepherd thinks it over. It's a big flock, so he takes the bet. The man replies, '973.' The shepherd is astonished, because that is exactly right. Says 'OK, I'm a man of my word, take an animal.' Man picks one up and begins to walk away.

'Wait,' cries the shepherd, 'let me have a chance to get even. Double or nothing that I can guess your exact occupation.' The man agrees. 'You are an economist for the Scottish Executive in Edinburgh,' says the shepherd. 'Amazing!' responds the man, 'You are exactly right! But tell me, how did you deduce that?'

'Well,' says the shepherd, 'put down my dog and I'll tell you.'

Edinburgh schemies love cats . . . they taste just like chicken.

'You seem to have more than the average share of intelligence for a man of your background,' said the advocate to a Weegie witness.

'If I wasn't under oath, pal, I'd return the compliment,' replied the witness.

Two Edinbuggers boarded a flight. One sat in the window seat, the other sat in the middle seat. Just before takeoff, a Weegie got on and took the aisle seat next to the two Edinbuggers. The Weegie kicked off his shoes, wiggled his toes and was settling in when the guy in the window seat said, 'I think I'll get up and get a beer.'

'No problem,' said the Weegie, 'I'll get it for you.' While he was gone, one of the Edinbuggers picked up the Weegie's shoe and spat in it.

When he returned with the beer, the other guy said, 'That looks good, I think I'll have one too.'

Again, the Weegie obligingly went to fetch it and while he was gone, the other guy picked up the other shoe and spat in it. The Weegie returned and they all sat back and enjoyed the flight. As the plane was landing, the Weegie slipped his feet into his shoes and knew immediately what had happened.

He turned to them and asked passionately, 'How long must this go on? This fighting between our cities? This hatred? This animosity? This spitting in shoes and pissing in beers?'

Q: What do you say to an Edinbugger with money?
A: Anything you like, he's not listening . . . and, if he inherited it, he can't even see you.

Edinbugger paedophile: 'You'll have had your sweetie.'

Even cheaper Edinbugger paedophile: 'Do you want to buy a sweetie?'

'What's this diet you're doing?' asked the Edinbugger of the Weegie.

'It's called the whisky diet, I've lost three days already.'

Glasgow recipe: Take a pound. Buy chips. Put salt and vinegar on them. Eat them.

Edinburgh recipe: Take a pound. Buy chips. Put salt and sauce on them. Eat them.

Glasgow saying: As cheap as chips.
Edinburgh saying: As dear as chips.

Two prisoners are talking about their crimes:

George: 'I robbed a bank, and they gave me twenty years.'

Jimmy: 'Hmm. I killed a man, and I'm here for three days.'

George: 'What? I rob a bank and get twenty years; you kill a man and get three days?'

Jimmy: 'Aye well, it was an Edinburgh lawyer.'

Weegies are even allowed to travel the world and in 1990 one was reported as being the only survivor of a plane crash when a jumbo went down in the South China Sea. The man was found clinging to a piece of board the size of a fag packet but had not been touched by the sharks which had quickly snapped up his fellow passengers. The Mate of the rescue ship was an Edin-bugger and when the Australian skipper of the rescue vessel expressed astonishment at the survival of the Weegie he pointed to the dripping, exhausted man lying flat on his back on the deck and said: 'See that T-shirt? It says "Glasgow: European Capital of Culture". Not even a shark is going to swallow that.'

An Edinburgh man, fallen far from his former station in life, is collecting for a tallyman. Up a close in Maryhill, the door is answered by a wee lad. The Edinbugger asks: 'Is your mother in?' and the wee man says: 'Naw, she's went tae the shoaps.'

'Och, laddie. Grammar! Grammar!'

'Aye, she's went wae hur.'

The National Poetry Contest had come down to two, a University of Edinburgh graduate and a Glaswegian schemie Hun. They were each given a word, and were then allowed two minutes to study the word and come up with a poem that contained it. The word they were given was 'Timbuktu'.

First to recite his poem was the Edinbugger. He stepped to the microphone and said:

> *Slowly across the desert sand*
> *Trekked a lonely caravan;*
> *Men on camels, two by two*
> *Destination: Timbuktu.*

The crowd supporting the Edinbugger went daft. Several murmurs of approval were heard.

The Weegie staggered up to the microphone and recited:

Me and this Tim stravaigin' went.
Met three burds in a tenement.
They wur three, and we wur two,
So I bucked one, and the Timbuktu.

At Queen St Station there was a man asking for his ticket in a strangely affected voice. A bear tapped him on the shoulder and demanded, 'You fae Embra?'

'Naw,' replied the guy in the same strange voice, 'I've just had a' ma teeth oot.'

Edinburgh District Council: so many fiddles going on that they hired Yo Yo Ma to conduct them.

Edinbuggers comb their hair in order to make an impression on the pillow.

People in Edinburgh equate breeding with good form, whereas in Glasgow they accept it as good fun.

Edinburgh ladies say things like: 'Oh Janet, he was just a bit too friendly . . . a real Weegie. He came up to me on the bus and put his hand up my skirt . . . you know the Jaeger one with the pleats.'

There is a fairly prevalent paranoid myth among Edinbuggers that all Weegies want to move to Edinburgh and drive down property values, just out of badness. One Weegie woman summed up her feeling succinctly: 'I wouldn't want to move to a place where you have to put on matching clothing to pick up the milk from the doorstep'.

Cultural fact file: There was a touring Scottish Opera production of Turandot in Glasgow in 1984. More people wrote letters to the then *Glasgow Herald* about it than bought tickets to it when it transferred to Edinburgh.

Glasgow has been described as savagely egalitarian, Edinburgh as civilised fascism.

A Weegie family are on a trip to Edinburgh Zoo. On the way back into town on the bus they find themselves behind a fur-coated Morningside lady, whose eyes rake them disapprovingly as she sits down with an almost audible sniff. The youngest child has one of those enormous drippy lollipops and is eventually wiping the drips off on the lady's collar. The Weegie mammy notes the lady's discomfort, just as she had noted the disapproval earlier, and says; 'Jasmine, stoap that!' then waits till she sees the lady relax a fraction before continuing: 'Ye'll get yer lolly a' hairy.'

5
WEEGIE FOOTIE

The Careers Officer is having a hard time interviewing a Glasgow pupil. 'What is it you want to do?' he keeps asking and the kid eventually says: 'Easy, peasy, Japanesy, Big Man. Ah'm gonny play fur Man U.'

The Officer is conscientious: 'Is that all you've thought of?'

'Aye.'

'Nothing else at all?'

'Naw. Ah'm a really good player, so ah mur, and I'll work really, really hard.'

The officer then asks: 'What if you're not good enough for Manchester United?'

The kid looks shocked: 'Ah mur so good enough.'

The Officer persists: 'But what if?' and the boy looks up defensively and says: 'Well, Cellik, then.'

'But what if you are really terrible and you are just kidding yourself or you get a bad injury and can only play a few games a season?'

The kid looks thoughtful and says with a shrug; 'Ah'd need tae settle for Hibs or Hearts, I suppose.'

Weegie question: Why does it cost more to get into Ibrox and Parkhead than it does to get into Easter Road or Tynecastle?

Weegie answer: Because, at Ibrox and Parkhead, sometimes there is singing and dancing.

The Weegie and the Edinbugger are arguing football and city merits. The Weegie is claiming that because no Edinbugger club has ever won anything significant in Europe, Glasgow is light years ahead and always has been, citing the Lisbon Lions. The Edinbugger claims that any selection from today's international assortment in Edinburgh would be better than and would beat the Lisbon Lions. The Weegie generously concedes that they might lose by the odd goal in three and adds: 'Mind you, most of them haven't trained for thirty-odd years.'

The Hibs scouts have been scouring the country, offering their usual sweeties and buttons for players and wages, but it is Knockback City all over the place. They finally find a youngster who looks very tasty and they get him to Easter Road for a trial, where he puts on an astonishing display. He then confesses that the surroundings have made him play

better, as he is a lifelong Hibbie, and says that he will play for no wages.

He is hustled into the office for a quick physical, but the doc eventually, as everything else is looking good, goes: 'Oh-oh.'

'What's the matter?' asks the lad.

'You're Jewish, aren't you?' says the doc.

'Aye,' he replies.

'Sorry, son, you'll not get a game here.'

'How no?' says the affronted boy, sensing persecution.

'Jesus, son,' sighs the doc, 'everybody knows that you have to be a complete dick to play for Hibs.'

6
STUPID EDINBUGGERS

The Weegie and the Edinbugger were on a parachute training course. The Edinbugger jumped first, pulled the rip-cord and started to float down. The Weegie followed, but when he pulled his cord, nothing happened. When he pulled the emergency cord, again nothing happened. As the Weegie plummeted past, the Edinbugger shouted, 'So we're in a race, are we?' and ripped off his parachute.

7
WEEGIE PHILOSOPHY, LANGUAGE AND SONGS

There are two golden rules for life in Glasgow: 1) Never tell people everything.

Glasgow is a sort of hybrid Highland/Irish town. Everybody knows what's going on, while Edinburgh comports itself more like a middle-class suburb of London, where nobody wants to know what's going on.

Hugh MacDiarmid didn't like Glasgow. He wrote:

> I'd call myself a poet, and know that I am fit
> When my eyes make glass of Glasgow
> And foresee the end of it.

But then MacDiarmid didn't like much.

A Tim sharing a train to the East with a Hun pal on their way to play Hearts and Hibs was heard to comment: 'No matter if we win or lose our games, we will still be winners in the game of life, because when they waken up tomorrow they'll still be from Edinburgh.'

Has Edinburgh ever had a good cartoonist who was also a poet? Bud Neill, a Weegie by choice, and much missed, wrote this:

> Winter's came,
> The snow has fell.
> Wee Josie's nosis frozis well.
> Wee Josie's frozen nosis skintit.
> Winter's diabolic, intit?

'By the way' – Billy Connolly has made this Glaswegian addendum to sentences well known around the world. 'That wis a right stupid thing tae dae, by the way' or indeed any other comment or observation can have this phrase added to it. So much so that other parts of Scotland sometimes

refer to Glaswegians as 'By the Ways'. A Weegie knows what he means when he says: 'By the way, by the way', okay?

I BELONG TO GLASGOW

Will Fyffe

I've been wi' a few o' ma cronies,
One or two pals o' my ain;
We went in a hotel, and we did very well,
And then we came out once again;
Then we went into anither,
And that is the reason I'm fu';
We had six deoch-an-doruses, then sang a chorus,
Just listen, I'll sing it to you:

Chorus

I belong to Glasgow,
Dear old Glasgow town;
There's nothing the matter wi' Glasgow,
though it's goin' roun' and roun'!
I'm only a common old working chap,
As anyone here can see,
But when I get a couple o' drinks on a Saturday,
Glasgow belongs to me!

There's nothing in keeping your money,
And saving a shilling or two;
If you've nothing to spend, then you've nothing to lend,
Why that's all the better for you!
There no harm in taking a drappie,
It ends all your trouble and strife
It gives ye the feeling that when you get home,
You don't give a hang for the wife!

Chorus

WEST IS BEST

We've come to Edinburgh from our city in the West
We've walked the length o' Princes Street and wurny
                              much impressed
We visited the Castle and we've done the Royal Mile
But gie us the Gorbals every time and Maryhill for style

Chorus

We're the boys, the bonny wee boys from Glasgow
We huv saw yer city and we think it's a fiasco
Aw they famous places that the Yankee tourists ask o'
Couldny haud a caunle tae Jamaica Brig in Glasgow

We went intae a restaurant tae hae a spot o' nosh
We didny understand them when they started talkin'
posh
A waitress came and asked us: 'Will you have it a la
carte?'
We answered: 'Naw, we think we'll huv a barra load
tae start.

Chorus

HOME AGAIN

Steven Clark

Open-toed sandals and it's pourin wi rain
I reach for my jacket as I get off the plane
It's great to be back after two weeks in Spain
It's great to be back home in Glasgow again

Home again, home again, jiggety-jig
Paris is elegant, London is big
Nae Eiffel Tower
Nae Millennium Dome
Then again, no place but Glasgow is home

Spring time in Glasgow and it's cold as you please
Snow on the ground and it's startin to freeze
No a flower to be seen, and it's zero degrees
April in Glasgow, no a leaf on the trees

Home again, home again, joggety-jog
Sydney has sunshine and Tokyo smog
Nae Bondi Beach here
But then again
The wee Clockwork Orange is our shinkansen

The wee guy beside me is just talkin shite
He's full of the bevvy and lookin tae fight
But I'm steamin too, so I very well might
That's café society in Glasgow by night

Home again, home again, jiggety-jig
Drunk as a monkey then sick as a pig
Home again, home again, joggety-jog
A big greasy breakfast then hair of the dog

Edinburgh's East, and Glasgow is West
Is Edinburgh better? Or is Glasgow best?
If ever I'm asked how to tell them apart
I say: One has a Castle, the other a heart

Home again, home again, jiggety-jig
For your Tattoo and Castle, I don't care a fig
You can keep yer auld Festival
– I don't gie a toss;
I'll take salt and vinegar, no salt and sauce.

I was brought up in Springburn, now most of it's gone
The place where I live now will never be home
You can never forget, no, nor ever disown
For Glasgow is bred in your blood and your bone

Home again, home, you can never go hame
The place you remember is never the same
Treasure the high points
Remember the low
And carry it with you wherever you go

Home again, home again, jiggety-jig
Paris is elegant, London is big
Nae Eiffel Tower
Nae Millennium Dome
Then again, no place but Glasgow is home

There is no Edinburgh song, Weegies sing, to the same tune as the Proclaimers hit: 'I'm fed up to the back teeth, with "Sunshine on Leith".'

Glaswegian definition of an atheist . . . a man who goes to an Old Firm game for the football.

Chief Weegie Billy Connolly, aka The Laird of Candacraig, should be declared a national resource, as he has been known to make even Edinbuggers

laugh, albeit a bit more slowly and less often than his hometown folk. Glasgow audiences see themselves as part as the show, Edinburgh audiences say: 'You nearly had me laughing out loud there.' Billy was in the Playhouse in Edinburgh when he said of the theatre, apropos of exactly nothing, as is his wont: 'Look at the size of it! You can get a licence to shoot antelopes in the balcony.'

Billy's attacks on Glasgow have been well documented and he has received criticism, not least from the Press, and it will be a wee while before he gets the Freedom of the City from the City Fathers, many of whom heard a joke once and didn't like it. But the jibes are funny, which is the point.

He called Drumchapel, where he did most of his growing up: 'A graveyard with fairy lights', and 'A desert wi windaes'.

Of Glasgow itself he has said: 'The great thing about Glasgow is that if there is a nuclear attack it will look just the same afterwards.'

He has also said: 'I was asked abroad why Glasgow never had a riot. But they did. It's just that it happened on a Friday night and nobody noticed the difference.'

Edinburgh's public schools are often blamed, probably because it is their fault, for the stiffness and emotional coldness which has led Glaswegians to dub Edinbuggers 'God's frozen people'.

There is a tale of a Weegie who shook hands with a Morningside matron, one of the ones with the husband called Elister, and lost four of his fingers to frostbite.

He is probably the same one who said: 'They never open their mooths till they've kent ye fur a week and then it's only to tell ye tae leave them alone.'

Casual Glasgow acceptance of immigrants:

'Wonder what their chips will be like.'

'I sometimes feel about as awkward as a left-handed violinist in a crowded string section, but let's face it, only a mediocre person is always at his best. At least I got one thing settled today. I spoke to the Duke of Edinburgh, who spoke to the Queen, and she's passed a law that if anyone beats Glasgow Rangers it's only a draw.'

Chic Murray

The Festival must never allow censorship to collapse
. . . it is far too good for the box office.

In Edinburgh there is a comfortable time-lag of a
century or so intervening between the perception
that something ought to be done and a serious
attempt to do it.

In Edinburgh real friends help you move. In Glasgow
real friends help you move bodies.

Edinbugger: 'Hard work pays off in the future.'
Weegie: 'Laziness pays off now.'

Glasgow saying: The Edinburgh gene pool would be
none the worse of a little chlorine.

Glasgow saying: He who laughs last thinks slowest.

In Edinburgh, a penny saved is a penny earned. In Glasgow, a penny saved is just stupid. What can you buy with a penny?

Weegie to Edinbugger: I've seen better-looking faces on pirate flags.

Glasgow saying: Ambition is a poor excuse for not having enough sense to be lazy.

In Edinburgh they say: 'Don't force it, ca canny.' In Glasgow they say: 'Get a bigger hammer.'

Edinburgh: Too many freaks, not enough circuses.

Edinburgh's suburbia: where they tear up the trees and then name streets after them.

Weegie threat to Edinbugger: 'Haw you! Off my planet!'

Nothing is ever a complete failure; it can always serve as a bad example. Look at Edinburgh.

As they say in Possil: Drugs may be the road to nowhere, but at least they're the scenic route.

Edinburgh City Council rule: If two wrongs don't make a right, try three.

Glasgow saying: Before you criticise someone, you should walk a mile in their shoes. That way you are a mile away from them and you have their shoes.

Glasgow saying: If you lend someone £20 and never see that person again, it was probably worth it. So chib his brother.

Glasgow saying: Dance like no one's watching.
Edinburgh saying: Don't dance. Everybody's watching.

Observation by a psychologist (an Edinbugger):

In Glasgow people put the lights on first, then draw the blinds.

In Edinburgh they draw the blinds first, make sure that no one can see in, and then put the lights on.

8
JUST DESERTS

A Weegie and an Edinbugger get into a car accident, and it's a bad one. Both cars are totally demolished, but amazingly, neither of them are hurt.

After they crawl out of their cars, the Edinbugger says, 'So you're a Weegie, that's interesting. I'm an Edinbugger. Wow! Just look at our cars. They're totally wrecked, but fortunately we're unhurt. This must be a sign from God that we should meet and be friends, putting our differences behind us.'

The Weegie replies, 'I agree with you completely, this must indeed be a sign from God!' He continues, 'And look at this – here's another miracle. My car is completely demolished but this bottle of whisky didn't break. Surely God wants us to drink this and celebrate our good fortune.'

Then he hands the bottle to the Edinbugger. He nods his head in agreement, opens it and takes a few big swigs from the bottle, then hands it back to the Weegie. He takes the bottle, immediately puts the cap back on, and hands it back to the Edinbugger.

He asks: 'Aren't you having any?'

The Weegie grins and then replies, 'No. I think I'll just wait for the polis.'

In Glasgow, to the traditional –

This is the tree that never grew
This is the bird that never flew
This is the fish that never swam
This is the bell that never rang

– has been added, because of the total and continuing failure of the mechanics of the much-touted feature of the new Science Centre:

'This is the tower that never turned.'

9
WEEGIES AND DRINK

Glasgow breakfast: A bottle of Buckfast, a pie and a collie dug. The collie dug is for eating the pie.

Glasgow compliment regarding a particularly fine whisky: 'It goes doon yer throat like a torchlight procession, bauns playin', the lot.'

Glasgow saying: There is no such thing as a large whisky.

The Weegie doctor checked over his patient and said with a puzzled frown: 'I can't really tell what the trouble is. I think it must be due to drink.' Jimmy said, understandingly: 'Ach, that's all right doctor. I'll come back when you're sober.'

In Glasgow a seven-course meal is a bottle of whisky and six cans of beer.

Glasgow saying: You aren't drunk if you can lie on the floor without holding on.

Glasgow proverb: Never drink whisky with water and never drink water without whisky.

Jimmy the inebriate Weegie was always coming home from the pub in the early hours of the morning. Eventually he found this note from his wife – 'The day before yesterday you came home yesterday morning. Yesterday you came home this morning. So if today you come home tomorrow morning you will find that I left you yesterday.'

Having returned at 3 a.m. from the office party, very much the worse for wear, Jimmy the inebriate Weegie woke his wife with a dreadful noise. She came downstairs to find him kicking the fridge and shouting: 'The cash machine isny workin'.'

A man called at Jimmy the inebriate Weegie's door collecting for the Home for Chronic Alcoholics. His wife answered the door and said 'Call back after closing time. You can collect my husband then.'

Jimmy the inebriate Weegie arrived at Sadie's flat with a carry-out of cans of beer and a bottle of whisky. After half an hour of chat, Jimmy eventually asked: 'When are the others coming for the party?' Sadie looked surprised. 'The party was last night. And you were here!'

An Edinbugger entered a bar and accidentally stood beside a Weegie, who immediately initiated a conversation. After they had chatted for a while the Weegie asked: 'Where are you from?' The Edinbugger replied 'I'm from the finest city in the world.' The Weegie lowered his brows and said with that indefinable aura of menace: 'Ur ye? That's no' a Glesca accent.' The pub was open again in a few days.

'Alcohol is your trouble,' said the judge to Jimmy the inebriate Weegie. 'Alcohol alone is responsible for your present predicament.' Jimmy the inebriate

Weegie looked pleased as he said 'Thank you, judge. Everyone else says it's my fault!'

When a tradesman finishes a job at a house in Edinburgh, it is an old custom to offer him a wee drink. 'Would you like a wee dram?' the lady of the house asked a Weegie joiner. 'Ah widny say no,' he replied.

The lady produced the bottle. 'How do you like it, Sandy?' she asked.

He replied: 'Half whisky and half watter. An' pit in plenty a watter.'

Alex the Weegie told his friends that he couldn't come to the pub because his wife was doing bird imitations – she was watching him like a hawk.

Callum the Weegie decided to call his father-in-law 'The Exorcist' because every time he came to visit he made the spirits disappear.

George the Weegie's long-suffering Edinbugger wife was fed up with her husband's unfortunate fondness

of a not-so-wee dram. Most evenings he would roll home from the pub considerably the worse for wear. His wife resolved to cure him. On Halloween, she put a bedsheet over her head, hid behind the hydrangea at the front door, and waited for her wayward man to come home. Eventually he staggered up the path.

His wife, in disguise, jumped out from behind the bushes, and cried out, 'George! I'm the Devil! And I've come to warn ye . . .'

'The Devil, are ye?' George interrupted. 'Then you must come in and have a drink with me, kinsman. I do believe I'm married to your sister.'

'Moderation, sir, aye. Moderation is my rule. Nine or ten is reasonable refreshment, but after that it is likely to degenerate into drinking.'

Anonymous, but definitely not an Edinbugger.

10
HEAVEN

An Edinbugger dies and goes to Heaven. He knocks on the Pearly Gates and out walks St Peter.

'Hello mate,' says St Peter, 'I'm sorry, no Edinbuggers in Heaven.'

'What?' exclaims the man, astonished.

'You heard, no Edinbuggers.'

'But, but, but, I've been a good man,' replies the Edinbugger.

'Oh, really?' says St Peter. 'What have you done, then?'

'Well,' says the guy, 'three weeks before I died, I gave £10 to the starving children in Africa.'

'Oh,' says St Peter. 'Anything else?'

'Well, two weeks before I died I also gave £10 to the homeless.'

'Hmmm. Anything else?'

'Yeah. A week before I died I gave £10 to the Albanian orphans.'

'Okay,' says St Peter. 'You wait here a minute while I have a word with the Big Man.'

Ten minutes pass before St Peter returns. He looks the bloke in the eye and says, 'I've had a word with

God and he agrees with me. Here's your thirty quid back. Now fuck off.'

In Heaven, there is peremptory rap on the Pearly Gates. 'Who's that?' asks Peter. 'It is I,' comes the reply. 'Haw Big Man,' yells St Peter to God, 'Is therr room furanurra fae Edinburra?'

A douce-looking young man knocks on the Pearly Gates and asks to be let in. St Peter says 'I don't know. Have you ever done anything good, like given money to the poor?'

'No,' replies the man.

'Helped a widow or orphan?'

'No,' replies the man.

'Helped a little old lady across a street?'

'No.'

'Well then, why should I let you in?'

'I did do something very brave once,' he said.

'And what was that?' asked Peter.

'I went to Glasgow on the Edinburgh train and ran around Queen Street station shouting "Weegies are all crapbags."'

'My, that is brave! When did you do that?'

'About three minutes ago . . .'

St Peter was manning the Pearly Gates when forty Weegies showed up. Never having seen any Glaswegians at Heaven's door, St Peter said he would have to check with God. After hearing the news, God instructed him to admit the ten most virtuous from the group. A few minutes later, St Peter returned to God breathless and said, 'They're gone.' 'What? All of the Glaswegians are gone?' asked God. 'Aye,' replied St Peter, 'and the Pearly Gates!'

11
HELL

One of the only two plumbers in Glasgow to charge reasonable fees* died and was sent to Hell by mistake. Eventually it was realised in Heaven that there was an honest Glaswegian plumber in the wrong place so St Peter telephoned (on the hot line, naturally) to Satan.

'Have you got an honest plumber there?'

'Yes.'

'He's ours, so can you send him up?'

'You can't have him!'

'Why not?'

'Because he's the only one who understands air conditioning. It's really cool down here now.'

'Send him up at once,' shouted St Peter, 'or we'll sue.'

'You'll sue?' laughed the voice at the other end. 'And where will you get hold of a lawyer in Heaven? They're all either here or in Edinburgh.'

---

*The other one is Jimmy Divers of West End Plumbers. Tel: 0141 946 6782

The preferred Weegie way of dying:

'I want to die peacefully in my sleep, like my grandfather. Not kicking and screaming like the passengers on his bus.'

12
LITERARY AND OTHER FIGURES

Various scribblers and scriveners have passed judgement on Edinburgh and Glasgow. Here are a few:

To imagine Edinburgh as a disappointed spinster, with a hare lip and inhibitions, is at least to approximate as closely to the truth as to image the Prime Mover as a Levantine Semite.

Lewis Grassic Gibbon: *Scottish Scene*

Isna Edinburgh a glorious city!

James Hogg

Aye, and totally wasted on its inhabitants.

A. Weegie

It's being sae cheery that keeps them going. See below:

> The Castle looms—a fell, a fabulous ferlie.
> Dragonish, darksome, dourly grapplan the Rock
> wi claws o' stane.
>
> Alexander Scott: *Haar in Princes Street*

To none but those who have themselves suffered the thing in the body, can the gloom and depression of our Edinburgh winters be brought home.

Robert Louis Stevenson

> EDINBURGH
> Your burgh of beggaris is ane nest,
> To shout the swengouris* will nocht rest
> All honest folk they do molest
> Sa piteously they cry and rame
> [*rogues or rascals]
>
> William Dunbar: *Satire on Edinburgh*
> (Or at least that is what he called the essay)

To promote a woman to bear rule, superiority, dominion, or empire, above any realm, nation or city, is repugnant to nature, contumely to God, a thing most contrarious to his revealed will and approved ordinance; and, finally, it is the subversion of all equity and justice.

John Knox, another Edinbugger who got it wrong, in the opening sentence of *The First Blast of the Trumpet Against the Monstrous Regiment of Women*

> A sacredness of love and death
> Dwells in thy noise and smoky breath.
> Alexander Smith: *Glasgow*

> City, I am true son of thine . . .
> From terrace proud to alley base
> I know thee as my mother's face.
> Alexander Smith: *Glasgow*

' . . . all the wise men in Glasgow come from the East . . . that is to say, they come from Edinburgh.'

'Yes, and the wiser they are, the quicker they come.'

Neil Munro: *Erchie, My Droll Friend*

It's Scotland's friendliest market-place
Watch your handbags, ladies, please.
   Gerald Mangan: *Heraclitus at Glasgow Cross*

Of a' the airts the wind can blaw
I dearly like the West
For there the bonny lassie lives
The lassie I lo'e best.
Robert Burns: *Of a' the Airts the Wind can Blaw*

An Edinburgh street song parodies this:

Of a' the airts the wind can blaw
I dearly like the West
It lends the Scottish Dyes a chance
And gies the Oils a rest.

The departure of the Wise Men from the East seems to have been on a more extensive scale than is generally supposed, for no one of that description seems to have been left behind.
   Sidney Smith, clergyman, essayist and wit, after a night on the swally with his Weegie pals.

Edinburgh is a city of ants, morose, frigid, and still preserving the same dread of spontaneous happiness and joy as in the days of John Knox, never content unless they are grumbling.

Tom Buchan, poet

Even Queen Victoria's man noticed that gay thing about Edinburgh, when she said in one of her letters: 'The view of Edinburgh from the road before you enter Leith is quite enchanting. It is, as Albert said, "fairy-like".'

Glasgow people have to be nice people. Otherwise they would have burned the place down years ago.

William McIlvanney, *The Papers of Tony Veitch*

Thou eunuch of language . . . thou pimp of gender . . . murderous accoucheur of infant learning . . . thou pickle-herring in the puppet show of nonsense.

West-coaster Robert Burns, responding to an Edinburgh critic, presumably after a snifter or two of the singing ginger

Edinburgh has two faces, one of beauty and order and the possibility of civilisation and the other of conservatism and the dead hand.

Glasgow is alive. It is full of hope and people wanting to be educated, wanting to try out something new, even if they don't rightly know what it is.

Naomi Mitchison

Alex Renton, not the Trainspotting one, had this to say of Edinburgh and its inhabitants:

'Perhaps it is the continual strain of trying to blend in with such a beautiful backdrop that leaves little time for the niceties of human intercourse.'

Robert Burns wrote to John Smith of Glasgow booksellers John Smith and Sons in 1787 thanking him after he had discovered that Smith, because of his admiration for the work of Burns, had taken only 5% in commission. He said: 'Ye seem to be a very decent sort of folk, you Glasgow booksellers, but oh, they're sair birkies in Edinburgh.'

Alexander Carlyle came to Glasgow University in 1743 after having been at Edinburgh. He commented: 'One difference I remarked between this university and

that of Edinburgh, where I had been bred, which was, that although at that time there appeared to be a marked superiority in the best scholars and most diligent students in Edinburgh, yet in Glasgow learning seemed to be of more importance, and the habit of application was much more general.'

13
MORE WEEGIE PHILOSOPHY

There is a tale of Glasgow etiquette concerning a couple. He says: 'Gies ower ma fags, ya ugly bitch,' and she says: 'Huv ye never heard the word "gonny"?'

Glasgow saying: No man is an island, except in his bath.

Quote from a Weegie architect: 'You just can't see Edinburgh building the Armadillo, can you? They don't even know what the word "gallus" means.'

Here's gallus: Two Weegies were captured by the Romans and imprisoned in a cell in the arena prior to being thrown to the lions. An instant friendship developed, as it does between Weegies, and they were chatting away amicably as they were led out in chains to the lions' den. They were thrown in and one was asking the other: 'So when is Jeannie's wean

due?' to receive the reply: 'Ah'll tell ye efter. Here's the lions comin'.'

And there is another lions' den tale of a posse of Possil kids on a bus trip to a safari park managing to escape from the bus and their guardians and prowl around outside among the animals. A keeper, concerned for their safety, came running over, shouting: 'The lions, boys! The lions!' to receive the reply: 'We never touched your lions.'

Glasgow saying: Edinburgh is the capital, but Glasgow has the capital.

It is a miracle that curiosity survives any formal education, especially the Edinburgh public school model, which may well have given rise to the saying: 'Glasgow people want to know, Edinburgh people think they know already.'

14
MOTTOES

The city motto: 'Let Glasgow Flourish', registered at the Lyon Court in 1866, is a curtailment of the text inscribed on the bell of the Tron Church, cast in 1631 – 'Lord let Glasgow flourish through the preaching of thy word and praising thy name.' There is a certain jauntiness and cockiness to the curtailment, is there not, and possibly an implicit threat. Perhaps: 'Let Glasgow Flourish . . . Or Else', or: 'Let Glasgow Flourish Or We Will Give You A Doing', is what was meant when it was shortened. The staid burghers of Edinburgh certainly seem to think so.

Although Edinburgh, like the other Royal Burghs of Scotland, used armorial devices on its seals and in other ways from early times and certainly from the 14th century, the 'achievement' or coat of arms was not formally granted by the Lord Lyon King of Arms until 1732. The arms were used by Edinburgh Town Council until the reorganisation of local government in Scotland in May 1975, when the council was succeeded by the City of Edinburgh District Council and a new coat of arms, based on the earlier one, was granted.

The description of the shield starts: 'The shield is blazoned as Argent, a castle triple-towered and em-battled Sable, masoned of the first and topped with three fans Gules, windows and portcullis shut of the last, situate on a rock proper.' The masoned bit is (of course) understandable and unsurprising (it is Edinburgh, after all) but the rest is incomprehensible unless you are Lord Lyon King of Arms.

The motto is (of course) in Latin, and is: 'NISI DOMINUS FRUSTRA', associated with Edinburgh since 1647. The interpretation is, 'Except the Lord in Vain', and is a normal heraldic contraction of a verse from the 127th Psalm:

> Except the Lord build the house
> They labour in vain that build it:
> Except the Lord keep the city
> The watchman waketh but in vain.

So Glasgow's motto is not only snappier, multi-layered, and understandable to your average punter, it is also older. Ha! I rest my case, whatever it is.

15
MEAN EDINBUGGERS

There's a modern twist to the old 'You'll have had your tea' Edinbugger statement. Apparently nowadays they gesture toward the drinks cabinet and say: 'Oh no, you'll be driving.'

An Edinbugger is someone who, when he or she has said 'You'll have had your tea,' and 'Oh no, you'll be driving,' and you have denied both, will, as they are dribbling you out a carefully measured modicum of cheap sherry and you say: 'Stop' out of politeness, does so.

When you ask for 'some mair', in Glasgow, they get you another drink. In Edinburgh, they open a window.

A Weegie, an Airdrieonian and an Edinbugger were in a bar and had just started on a new round of drinks when a fly landed in each glass of beer. The

Weegie took his out on the blade of his knife. The Airdrieonian picked his out and put it in his bottle of Buckfast for later. The Edinbugger lifted his one up carefully by the wings and held it above his glass, saying: 'Go on, spit it out.'

George the crafty Edinbugger had become a bit hard of hearing, but he didn't want to pay for a hearing aid. So he bought a piece of flex, put one end in his top pocket and the other end in his ear. It didn't help his hearing but he found that people spoke to him more loudly.

An Edinbugger matron, who was rather stingy with her whisky, was giving a drink to a tradesman who had done a good job. As she handed him his glass, she said it was good whisky, being fourteen years old. 'Aye, well, Mrs,' said the man, regarding his glass sorrowfully, 'it's very small for its age.'

George the careful Edinbugger took his girlfriend out for the evening. They returned to her flat just before midnight and as she kissed him goodnight she said: 'Be careful on your way home. I'd hate

anyone to rob you of all the money you've saved this evening.'

There was understandable scepticism when it was suggested that Napoleon Bonaparte was the grandson of an Edinbugger from Morningside. But now it has been pointed out that there is further proof that Napoleon was indeed from the East – apart from being a wee loser, his hand was always under his jacket, to make sure no-one had lifted his wallet. . .

A visitor to an Edinburgh bar was surprised to find the beer only two pence a pint. The barman explained that it was a special price to mark the centenary of the pub opening. The visitor noticed, however, that the bar was empty. 'Are the regular customers not enjoying the special prices?' he asked. To which the barman replied: 'They're waiting for the Happy Hour.'

It is rumoured that the entire population of Edinburgh took to the streets with an empty glass in their hands when the weather forecaster said there would be a nip in the air.

How do you persuade an Edinbugger to go on the roof? Tell him the drinks are on the house . . .

When a bus company was prevailed upon to increase the concessionary fare to frequent travellers so that they got six journeys instead of four for a pound, one elderly Morningside gentleman, renowned for his frugality, even in a community where frugal folk are common, was still unhappy.

'It's all dam' foolishness,' he declared. 'Now we've got to walk to town six times instead of four times to save a pound!'

Did you hear about the Edinbugger who got caught making nuisance telephone calls? He kept reversing the charges.

A Glasgow prayer: 'Oh Lord, we do not ask you to give us wealth. Just show us where it is.'

An Edinburgh prayer: 'Oh Lord, we do not ask you to give us wealth. Just show us where the Weegies are.'

Edinburgh bureaucrats: A difficulty for every solution.

Angus called in to see his Edinbugger friend Donald to find he was stripping the wallpaper from the walls. Rather obviously, he remarked, 'You're decorating, I see,' to which Donald replied, 'No. I'm moving house.' If he had been a Weegie he would have been kidding.

Have you heard the rumour that the Grand Canyon was started by an Edinbugger who dropped a penny in a ditch?

Hear the one about the Edinbugger who went out into the close the night before Christmas, blew up and burst a paper bag, and then told his kids that Santa had committed suicide?

Hear the one about the Edinbugger who flew to Norway at enormous expense (in his eyes) and was sitting on a pier in Oslo when a diver came to the surface, removed his headgear, lit a cigarette, and

said: 'Howzitgaun?' The Edinbugger replied: 'If I'd known you could walk it I'd have beaten you here.'

Hear the one about the Edinbugger who whispered to one of the Siamese twins, 'Get rid of your sister, an' I'll stand you a drink'?

An Edinbugger wrote to an editor, 'If you don't stop printing derogatory jokes about mean-spirited East-coasters, I'll stop borrowing your damn magazine.'

After discovering that they had won £15 million in the Lottery, Mr and Mrs McEdinbugger sat down to discuss their future. Mrs McEdinbugger announced, 'After twenty years of washing other people's stairs, I can throw my old scrubbing brush away at last.' Her husband agreed – 'Of course you can, pet. We can easily afford to buy you a new one now.'

Edinbuggers have an infallible cure for sea-sickness. They lean over the side of the ship with a ten pence coin in their teeth.

In some Edinburgh restaurants they heat the knives so you can't use too much butter. In Glasgow restaurants the knives are chained to the tables. With very short chains.